MARVEL

WOLVERINE™ VS SABRETOOTH™

Based on the Marvel comic book series **Wolverine**
Adapted by **Clarissa S. Wong**
Illustrated by **Val Semeiks** *and* **Hi-Fi Design**

Published by Marvel Press, an imprint of Disney Book Group. No part of this book may be reproduced or transmitted in any form or by any means, electronic or mechanical, including photocopying, recording, or by any information storage and retrieval system, without written permission from the publisher.

For information address Marvel Press, 114 Fifth Avenue, New York, New York 10011-5690.
Printed in the United States of America
First Edition
1 3 5 7 9 10 8 6 4 2
G658-7729-4-12349
ISBN 978-1-4231-7289-5

marvelkids.com

MARVEL
New York

MW00898044

All of the **X-Men** were hiding in a room in the Xavier mansion. They were getting ready for Wolverine's surprise birthday party. Storm and Angel bought balloons, and Cyclops and Marvel Girl got a birthday cake.

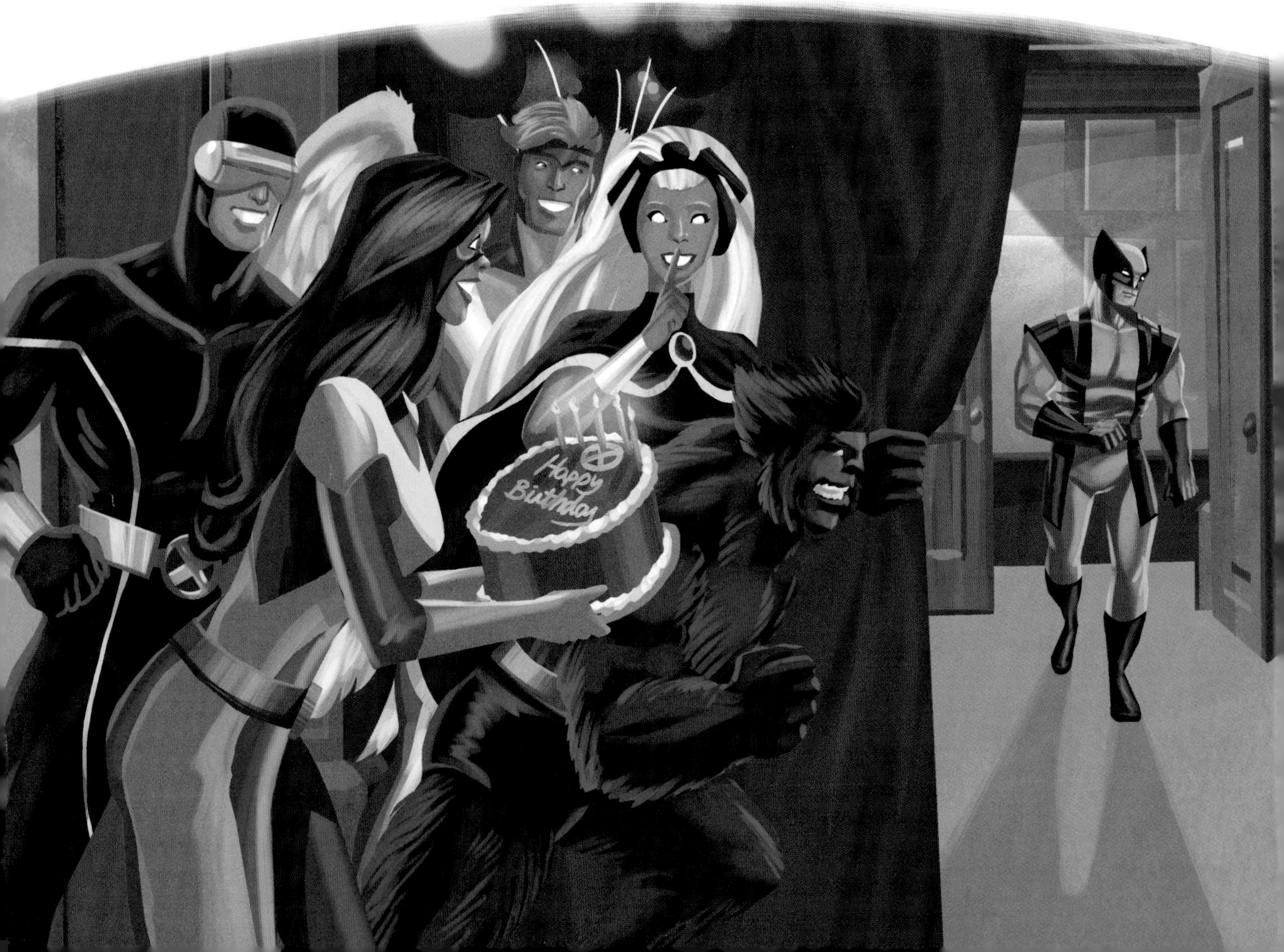
Happy Birthday

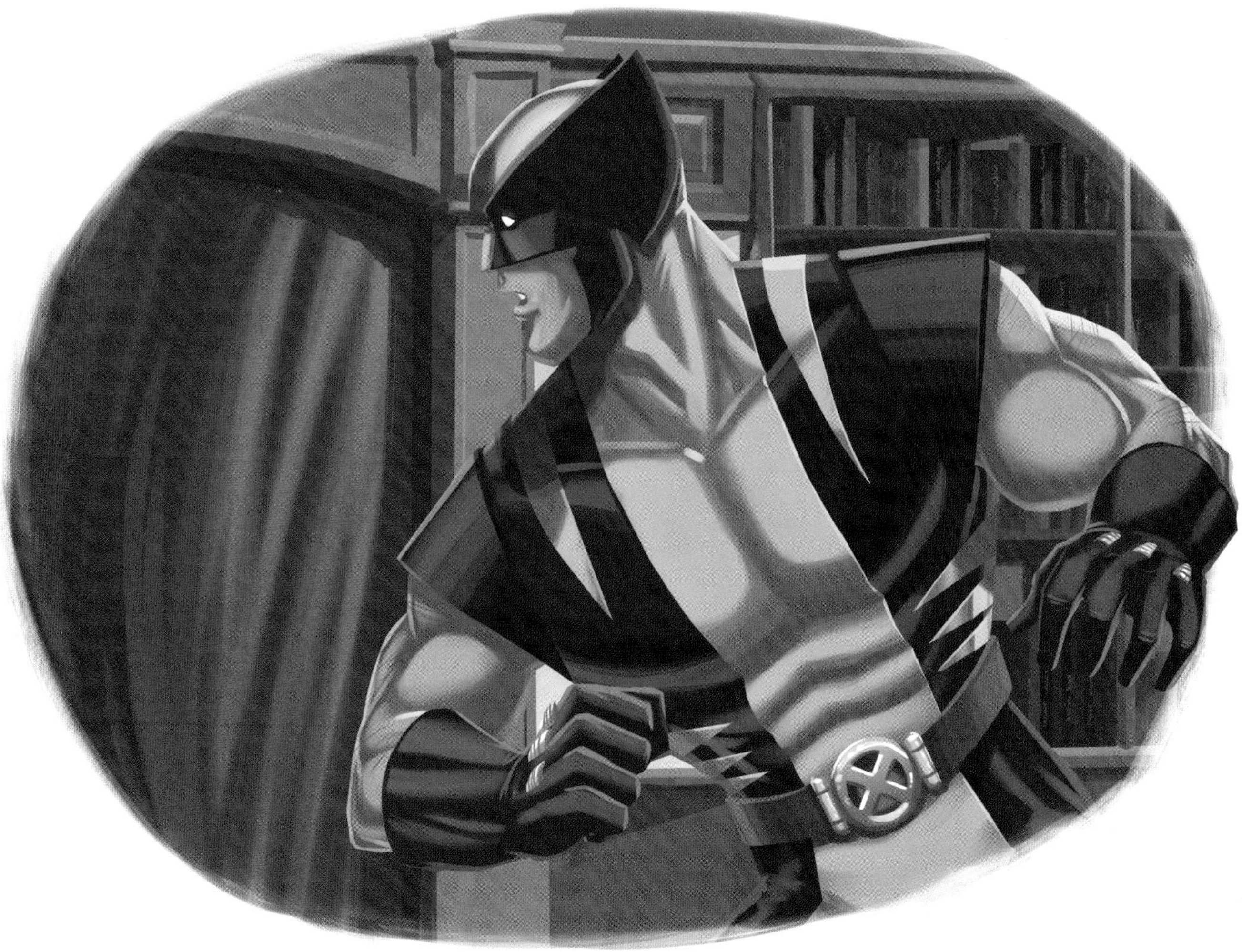

But Wolverine thought someone was sneaking into the mansion! Whoever it was, he had to **stop them.**

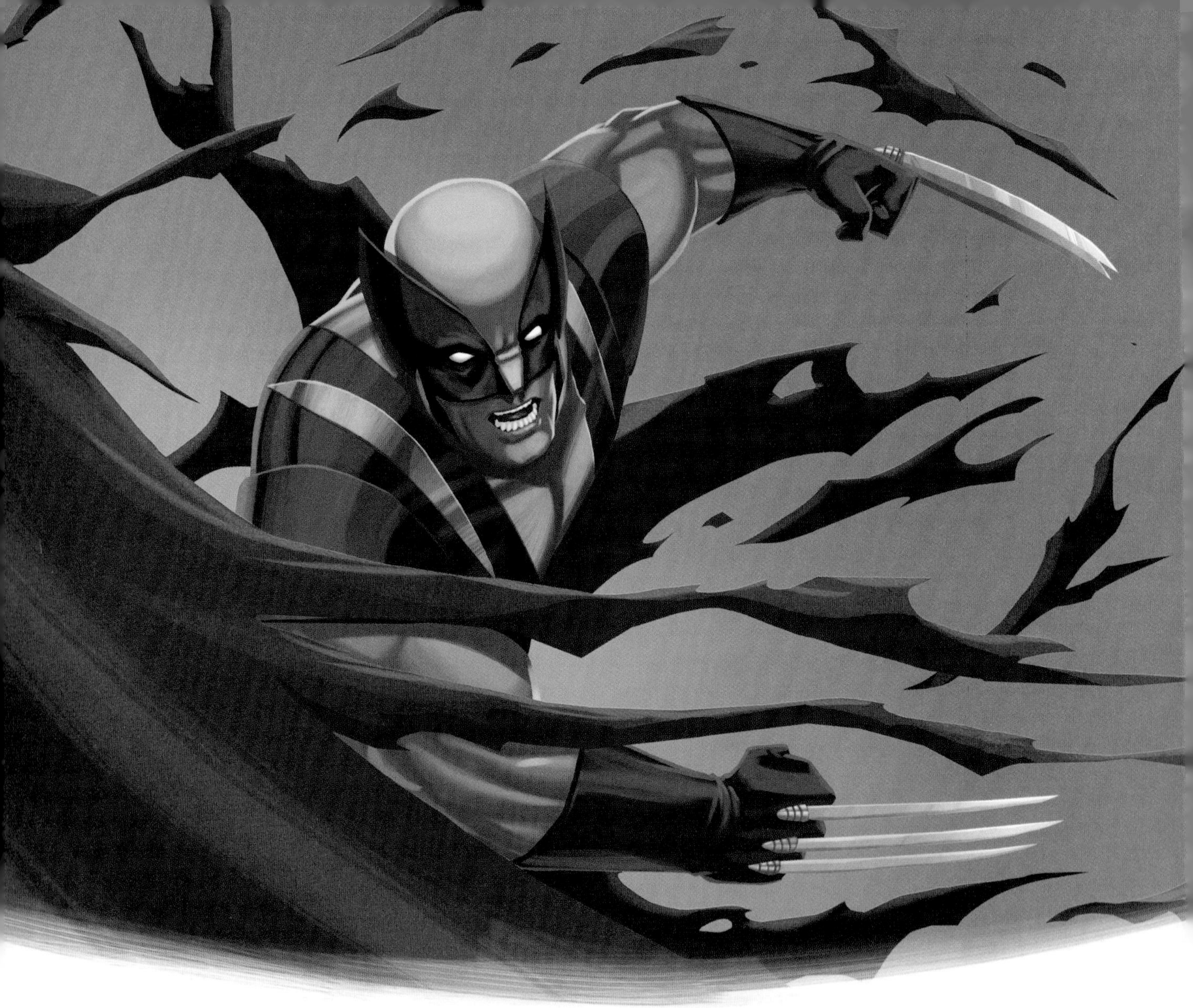

So he did what he does best. **He charged into the room** with his claws out!

As Wolverine clawed through the curtain, he was surprised to see all his friends. The other X-Men were even more surprised by Wolverine's attack.

"What's going on here?" Wolverine asked, confused.

"We were throwing you a surprise party. . ." Beast started.

". . .and that was your birthday cake. I hope you liked it," Marvel Girl explained.

Wolverine had always worried that he didn't fit in with the rest of the X-Men. Ruining his own birthday party made him sure of it, and he wanted to get away.

He jumped on his motorcycle and traveled all the way to Canada. He wanted to be alone in the wilderness, where the air was crisp and there was not a single soul in sight.

But hehad the feeling that **someone** was following him.

Wolverine traveled into a mountain range. When he reached the top of the mountain, his instincts were telling him someone was still watching him. He looked around and saw someone running at him, and fast!

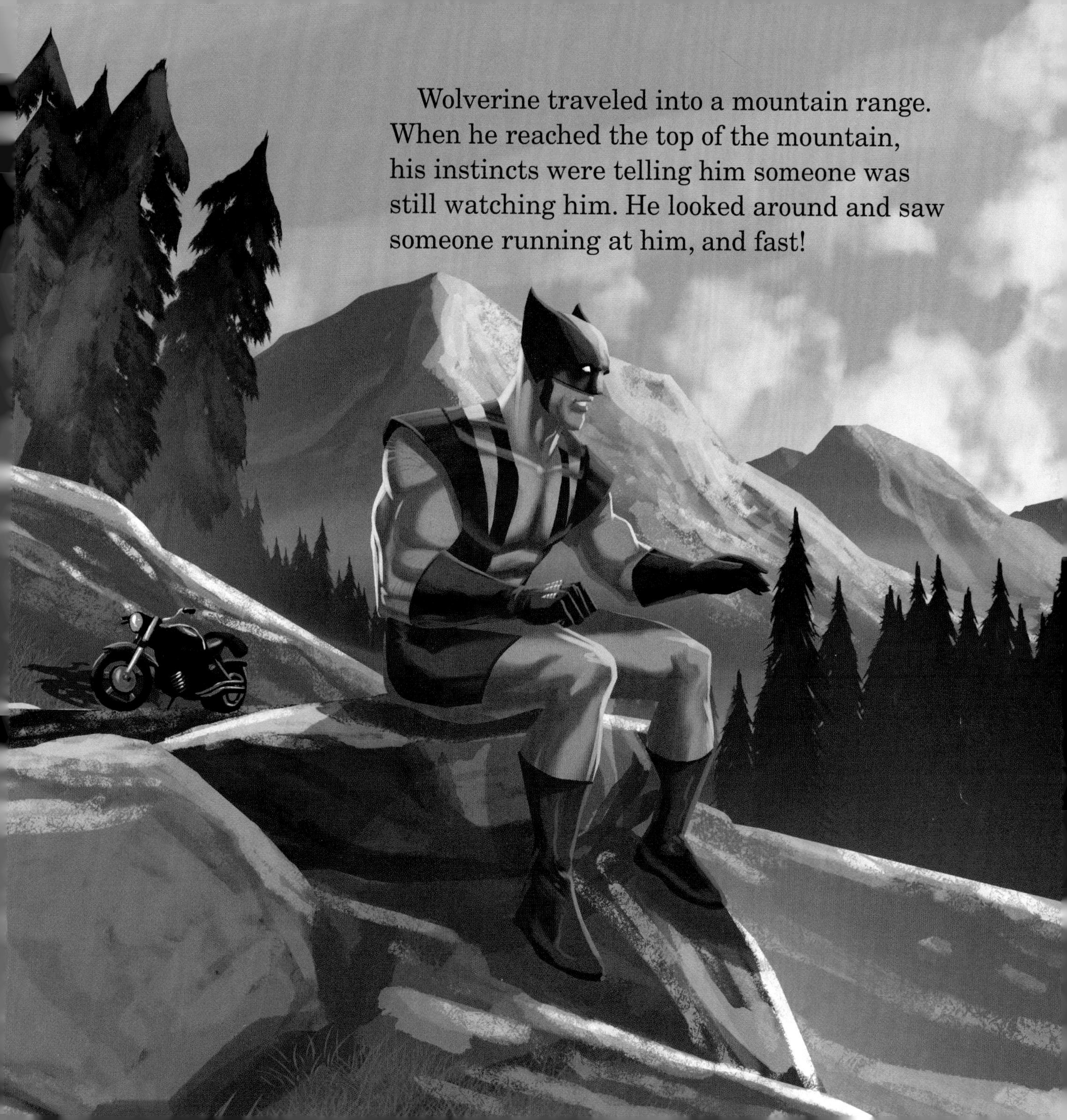

A giant man with sharp claws lunged out from the darkness. He knocked Wolverine off his feet!

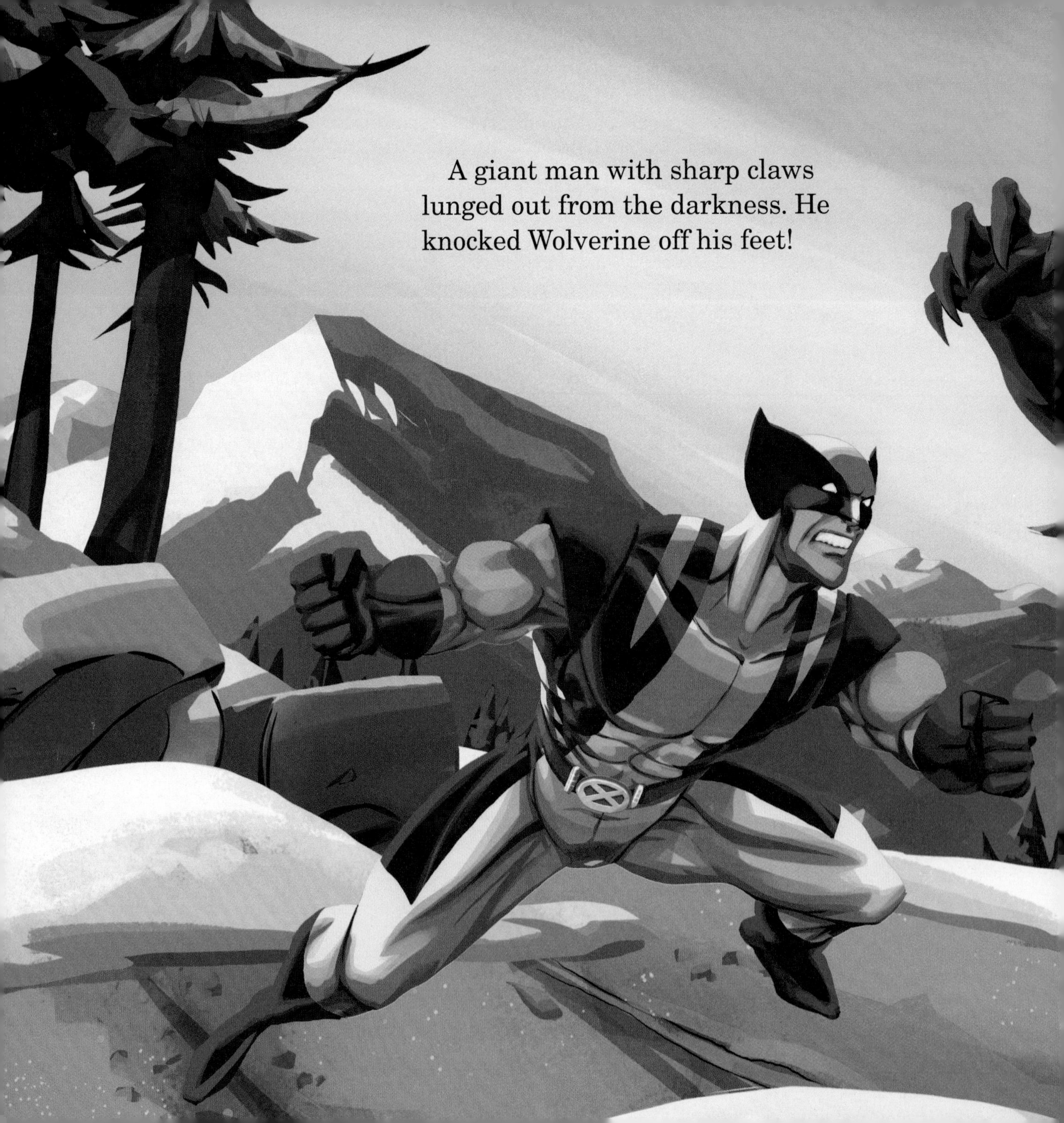

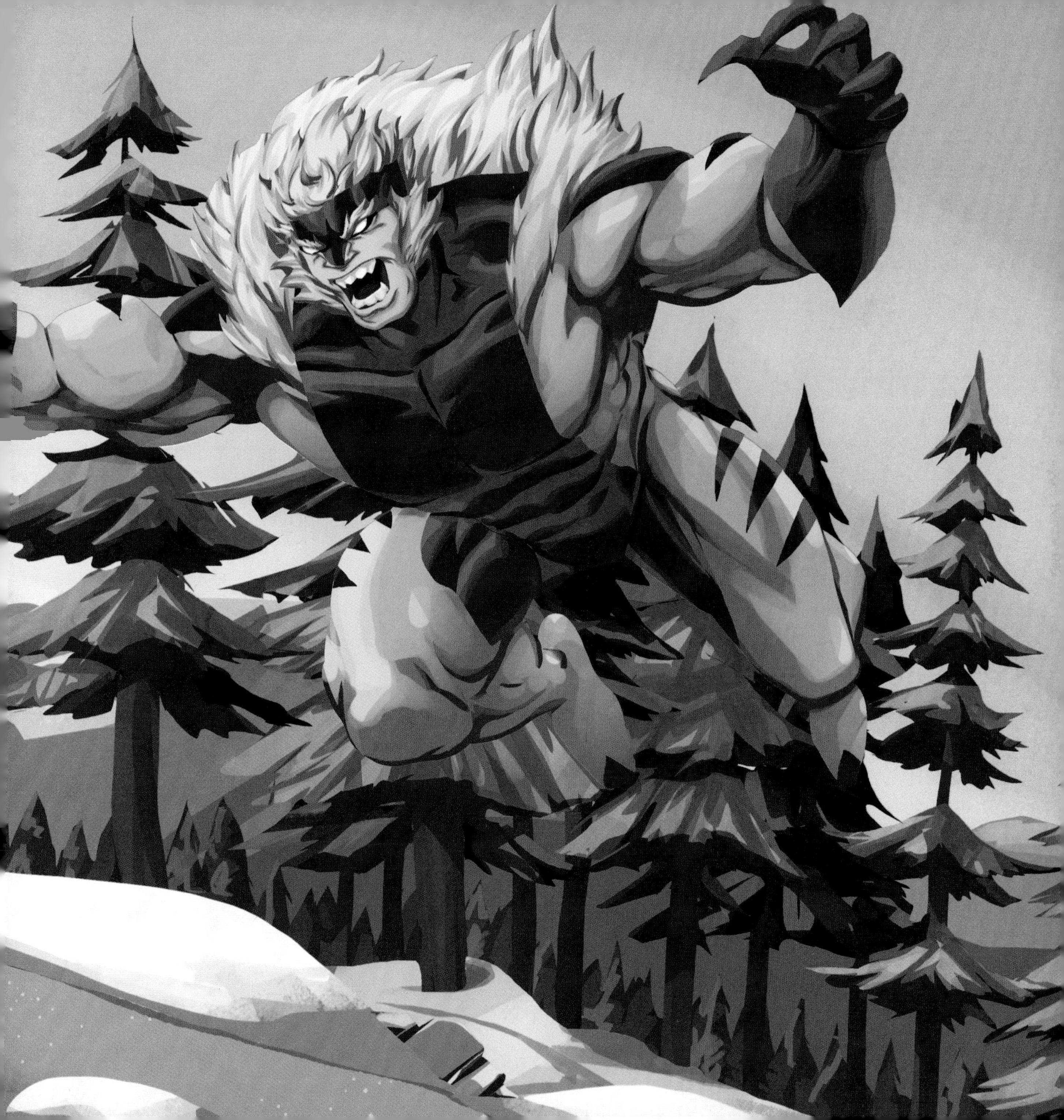

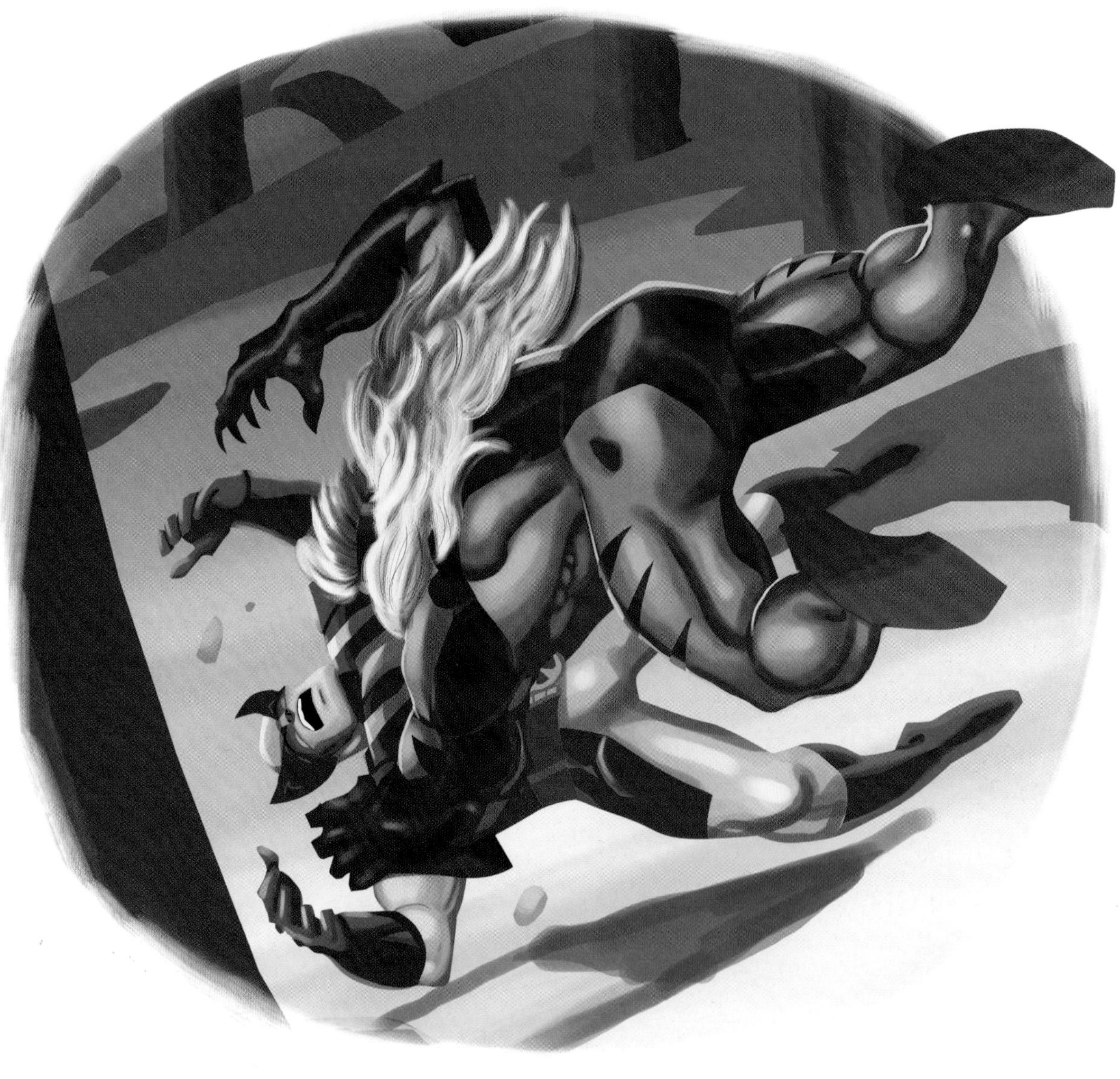

"Who are you?" Wolverine asked as the two men wrestled. "What do you want?" Wolverine asked as the two men wrestled.

"You don't remember me, do you? Well I remember *you*. . .Logan," the strange man said with a sinister smirk. **"Sorry** I missed the party, but I wanted to wish you a happy birthday!"

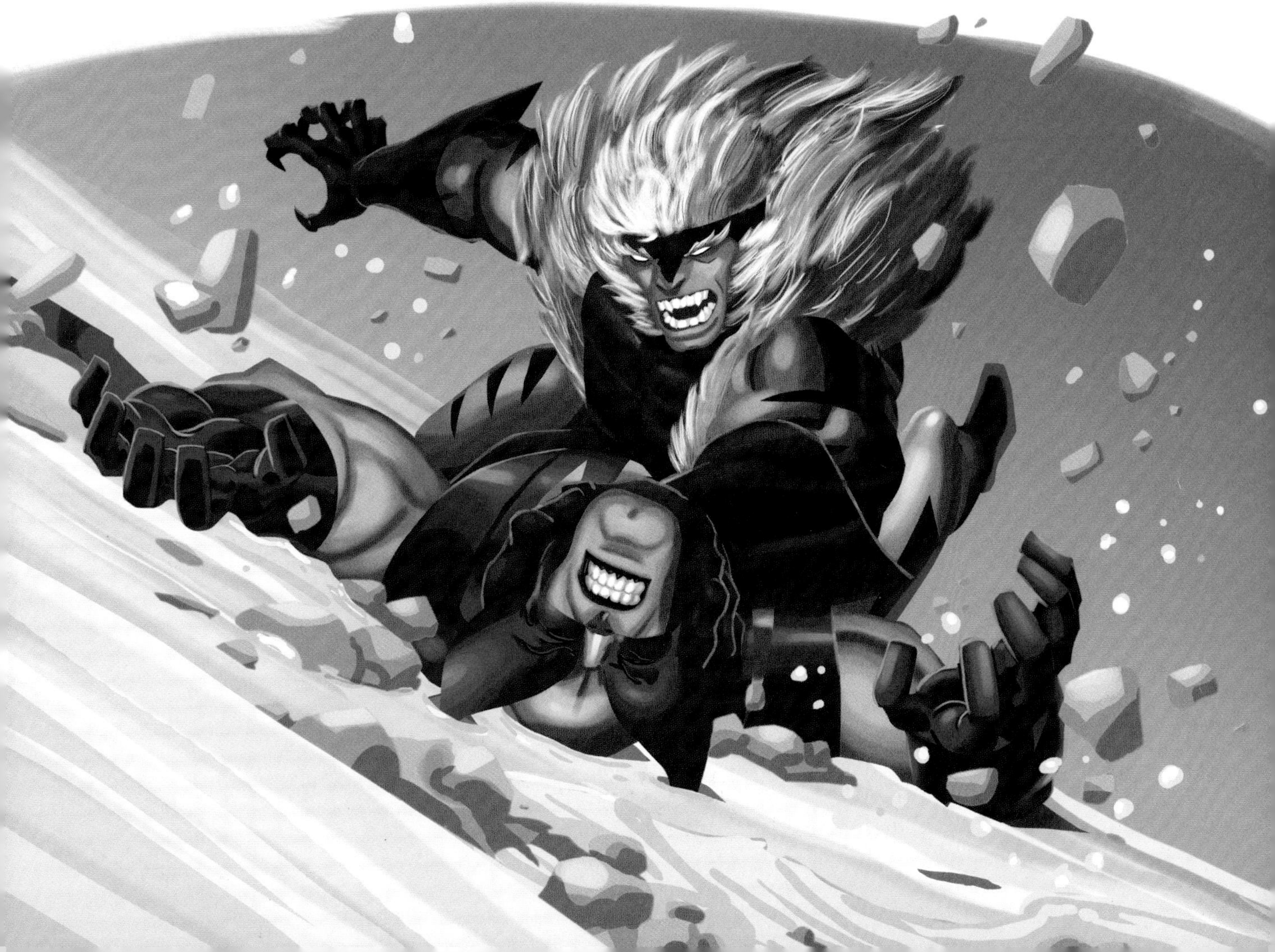

How does he know my name? Wolverine thought. Why is he fighting me? Wolverine finally managed to shake his enemy off, giving him enough time to unleash his powerful claws.

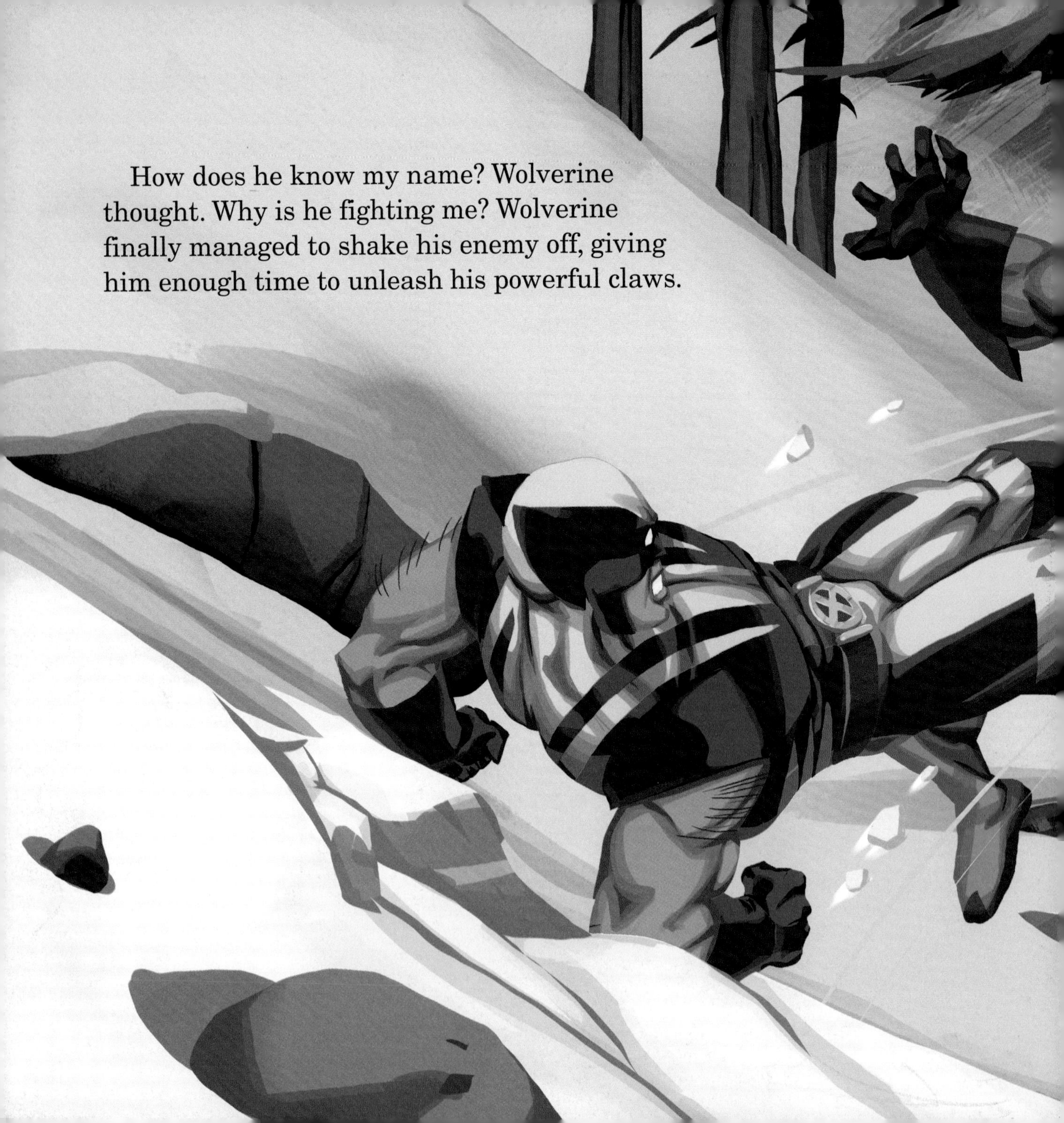

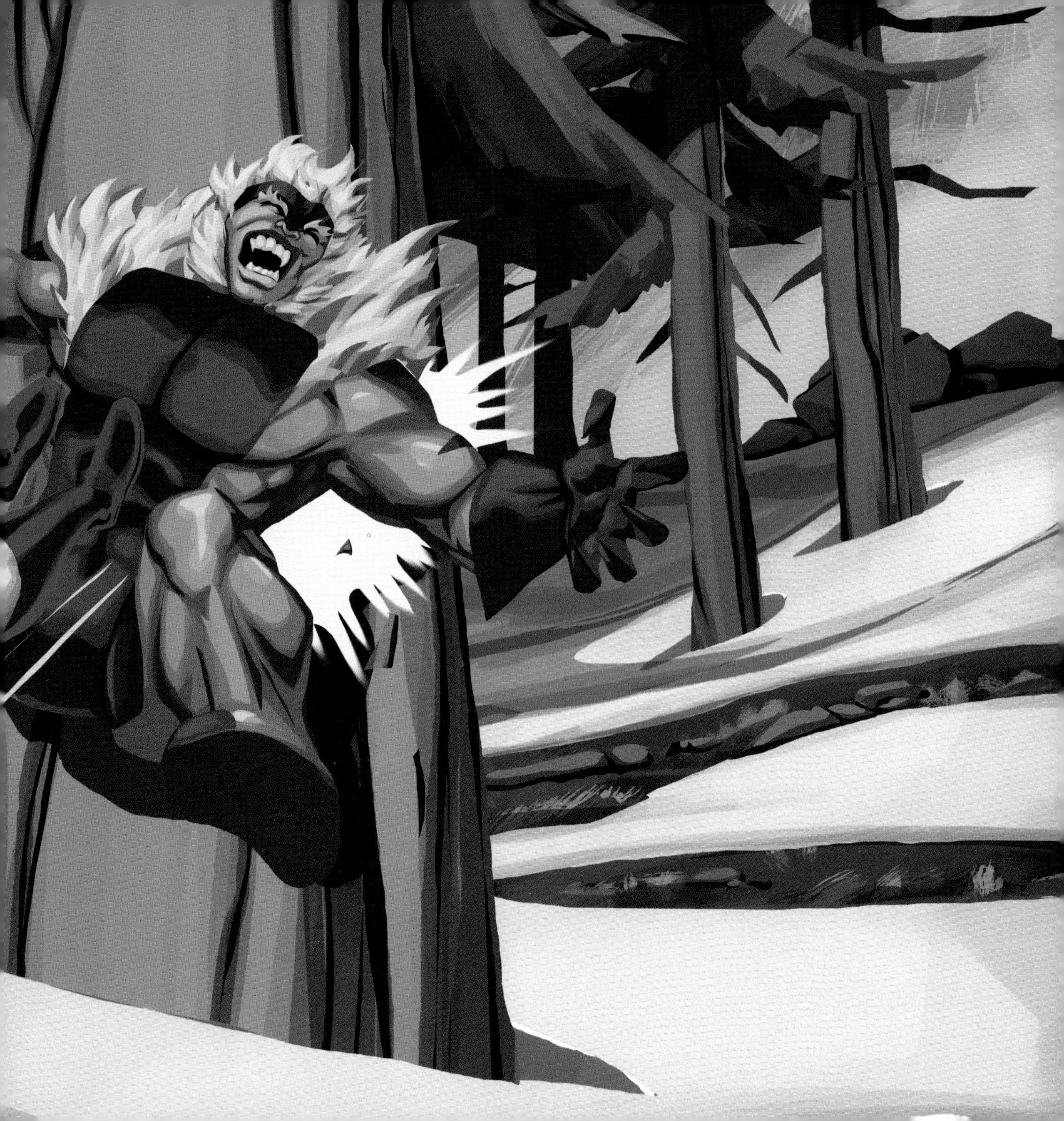

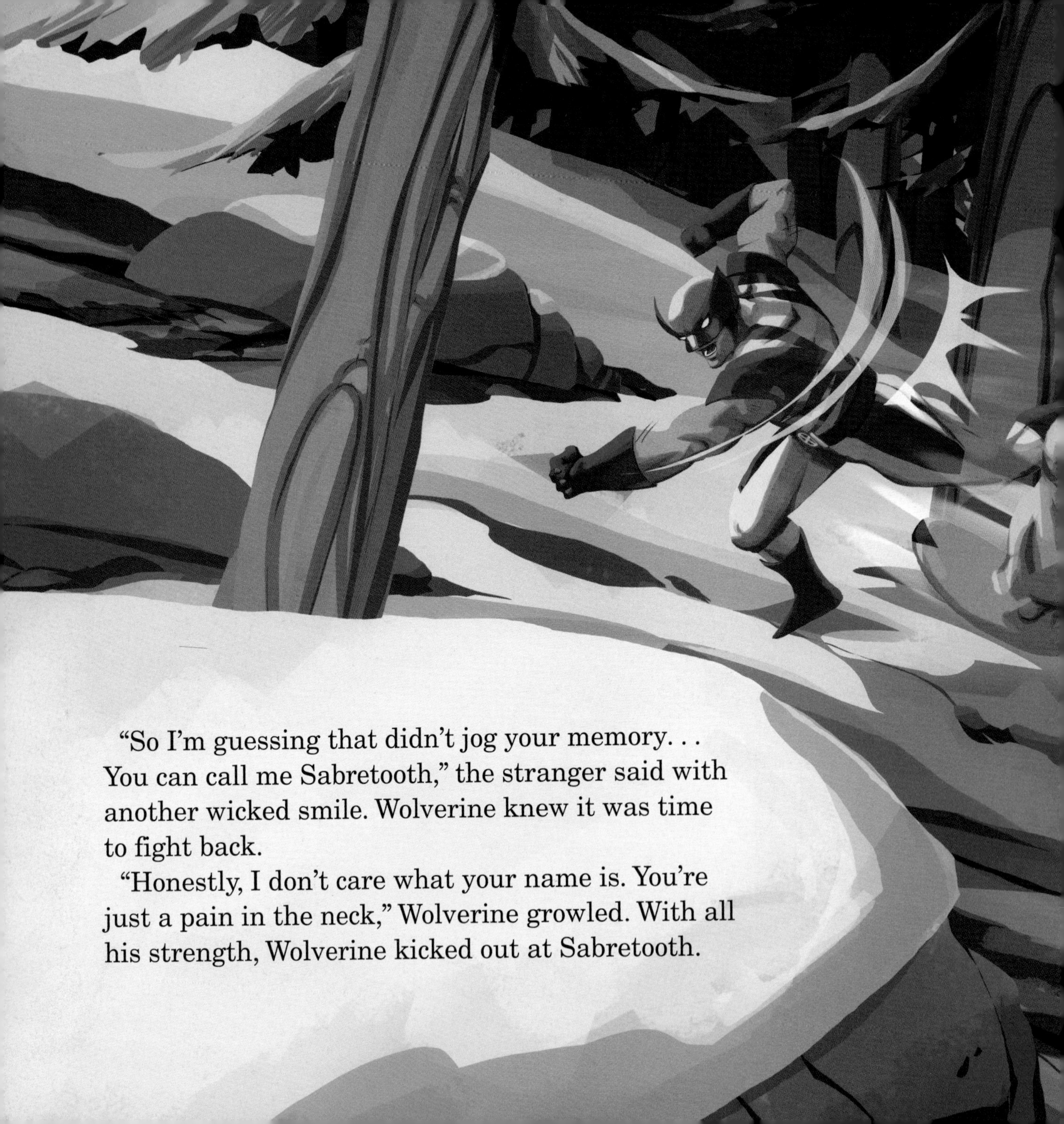

“So I’m guessing that didn’t jog your memory. . . You can call me Sabretooth,” the stranger said with another wicked smile. Wolverine knew it was time to fight back.

“Honestly, I don’t care what your name is. You’re just a pain in the neck,” Wolverine growled. With all his strength, Wolverine kicked out at Sabretooth.

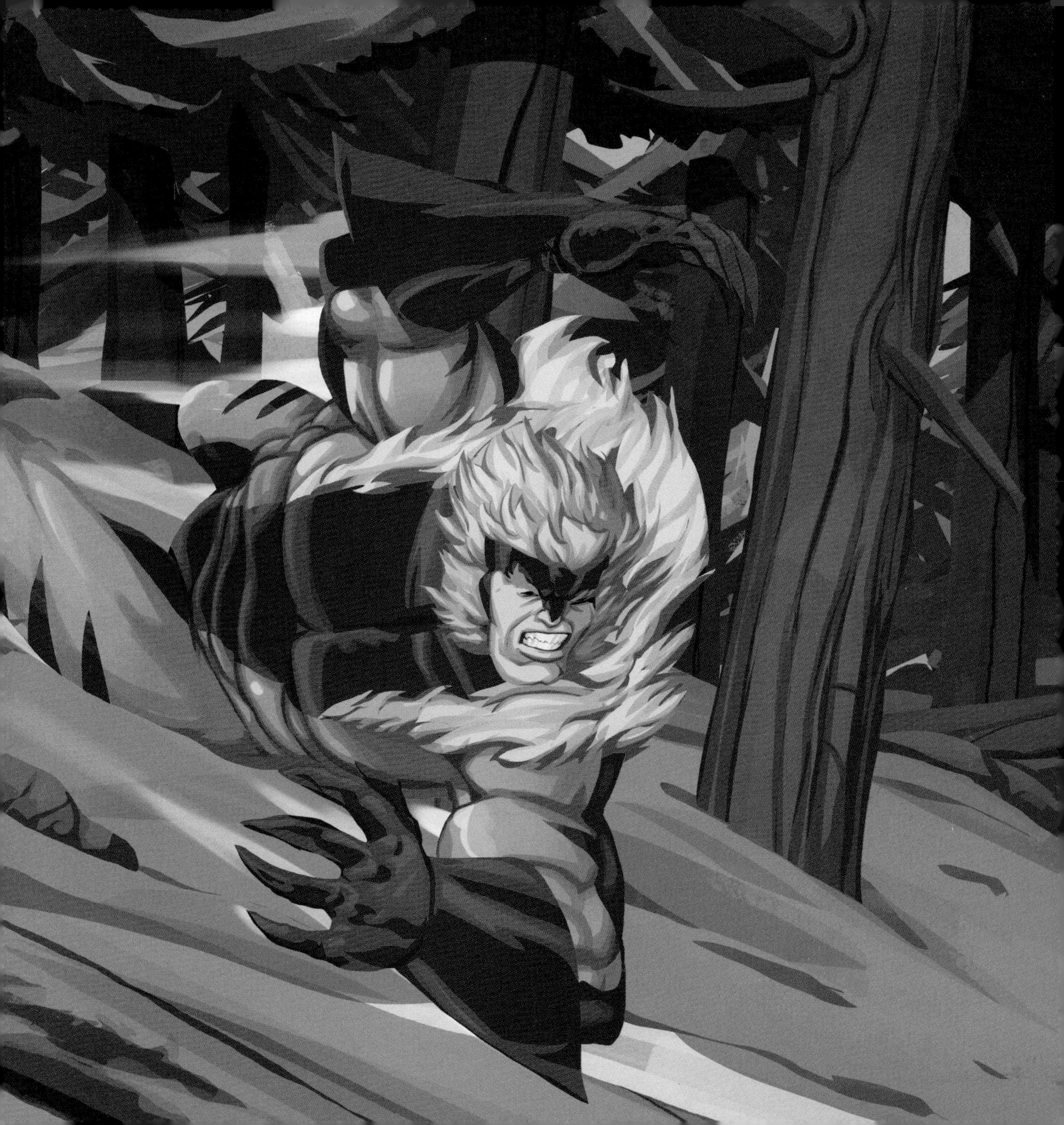

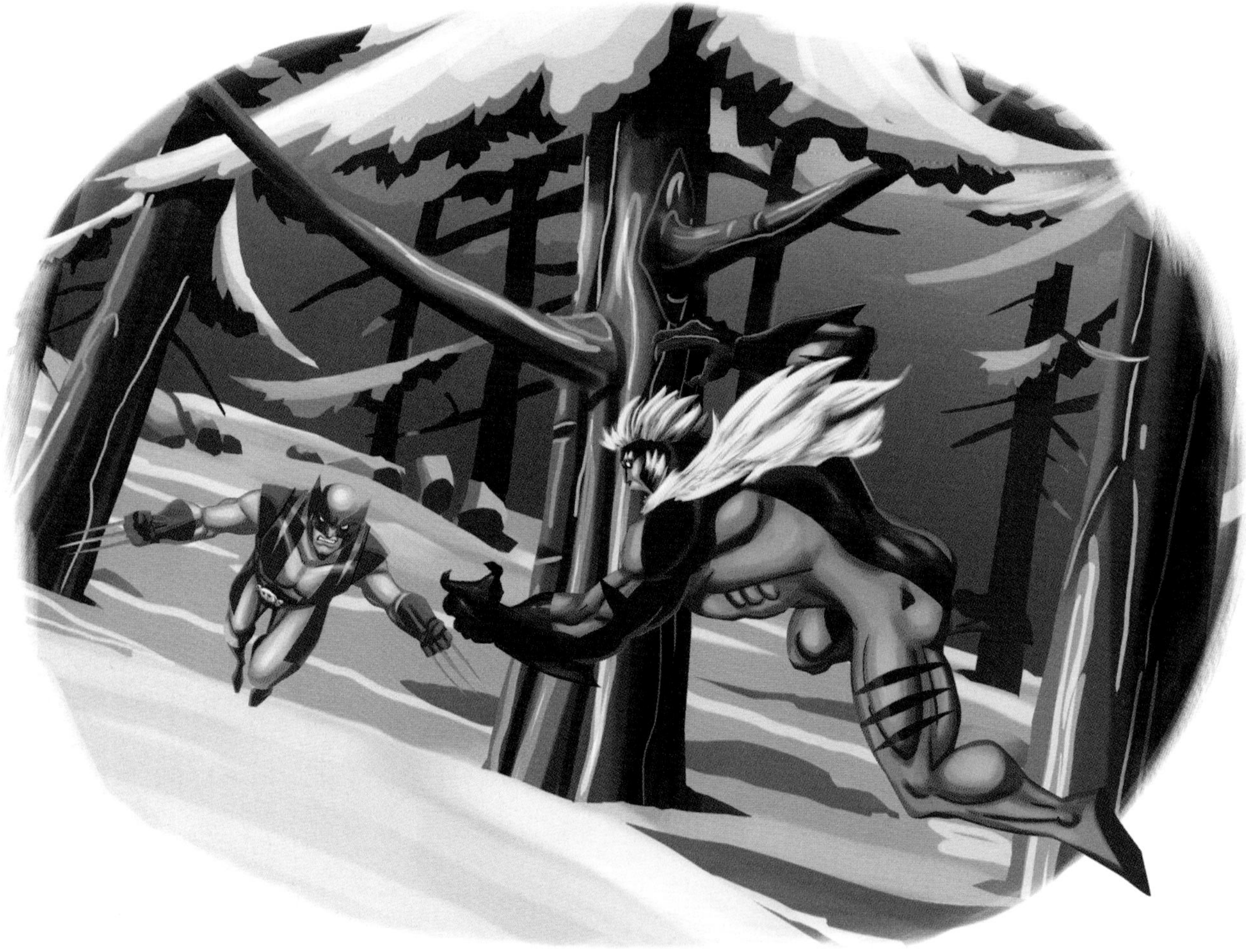

Despite his size, Sabretooth was quick, and he ducked out of the way. Sabretooth was just as strong and fast as Wolverine. Wolverine quickly noticed Sabretooth was a mutant. The villain had the same healing power as Wolverine! The only **difference** between the two was the wild look in Sabretooth's eyes.

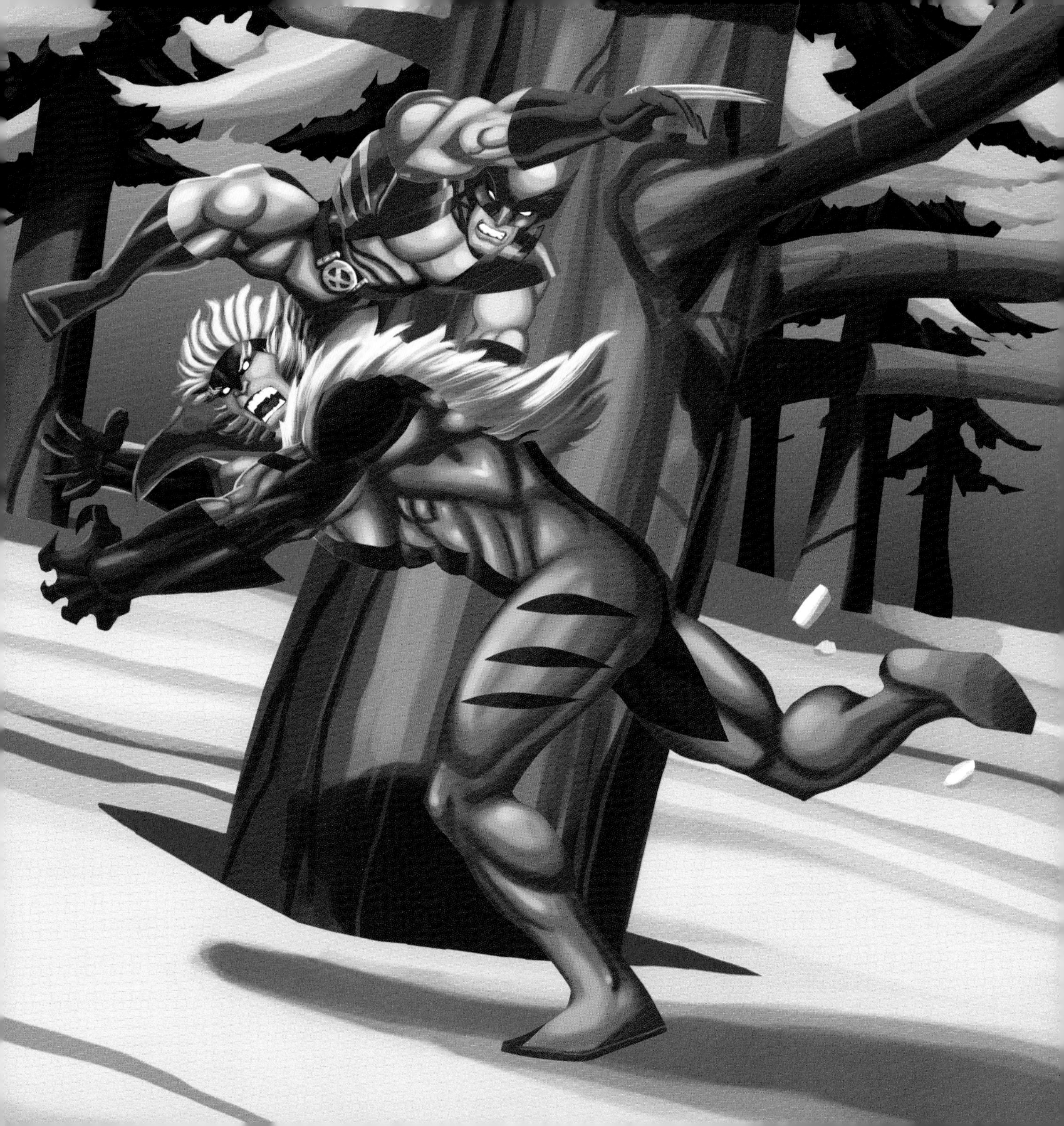

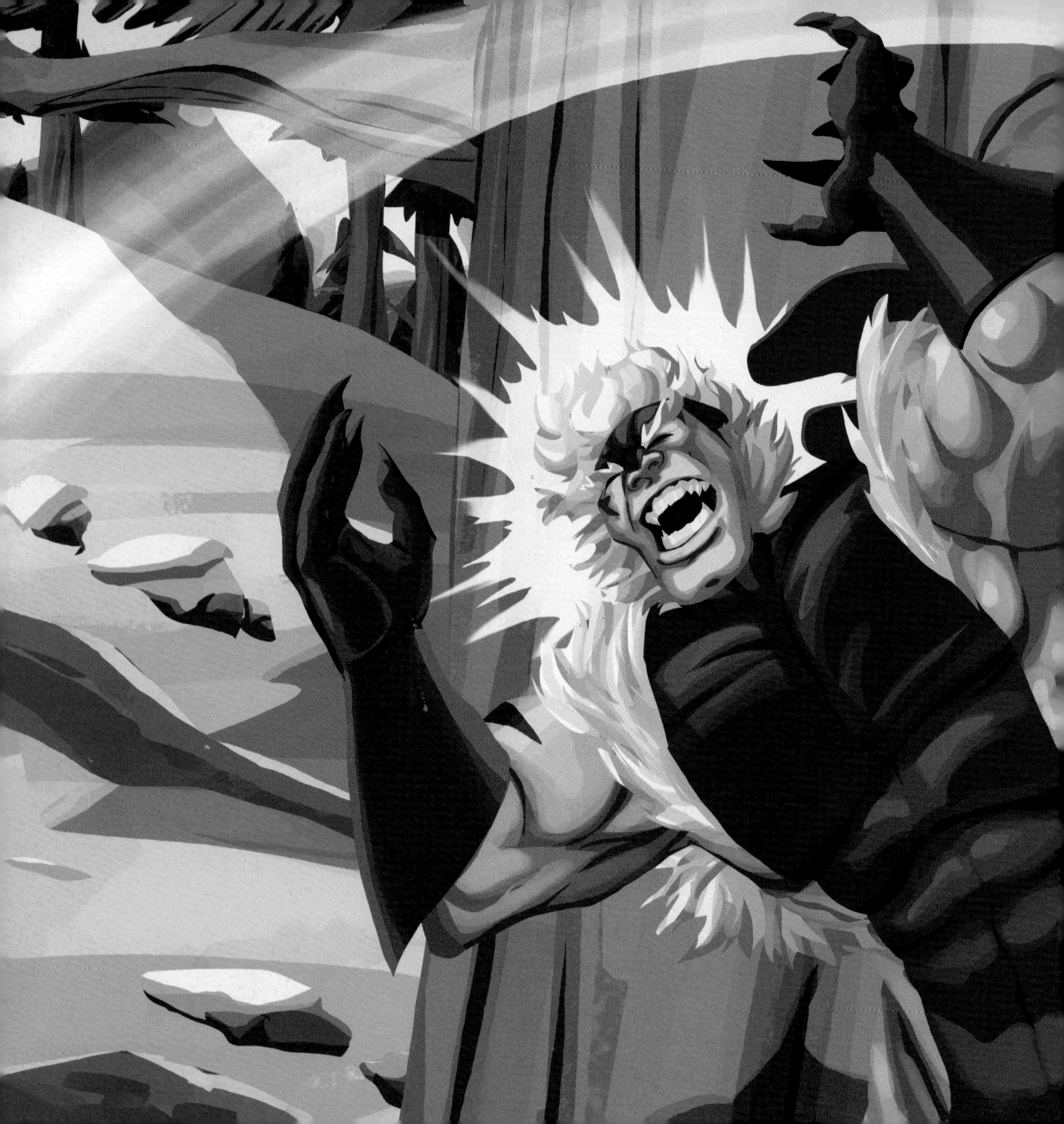

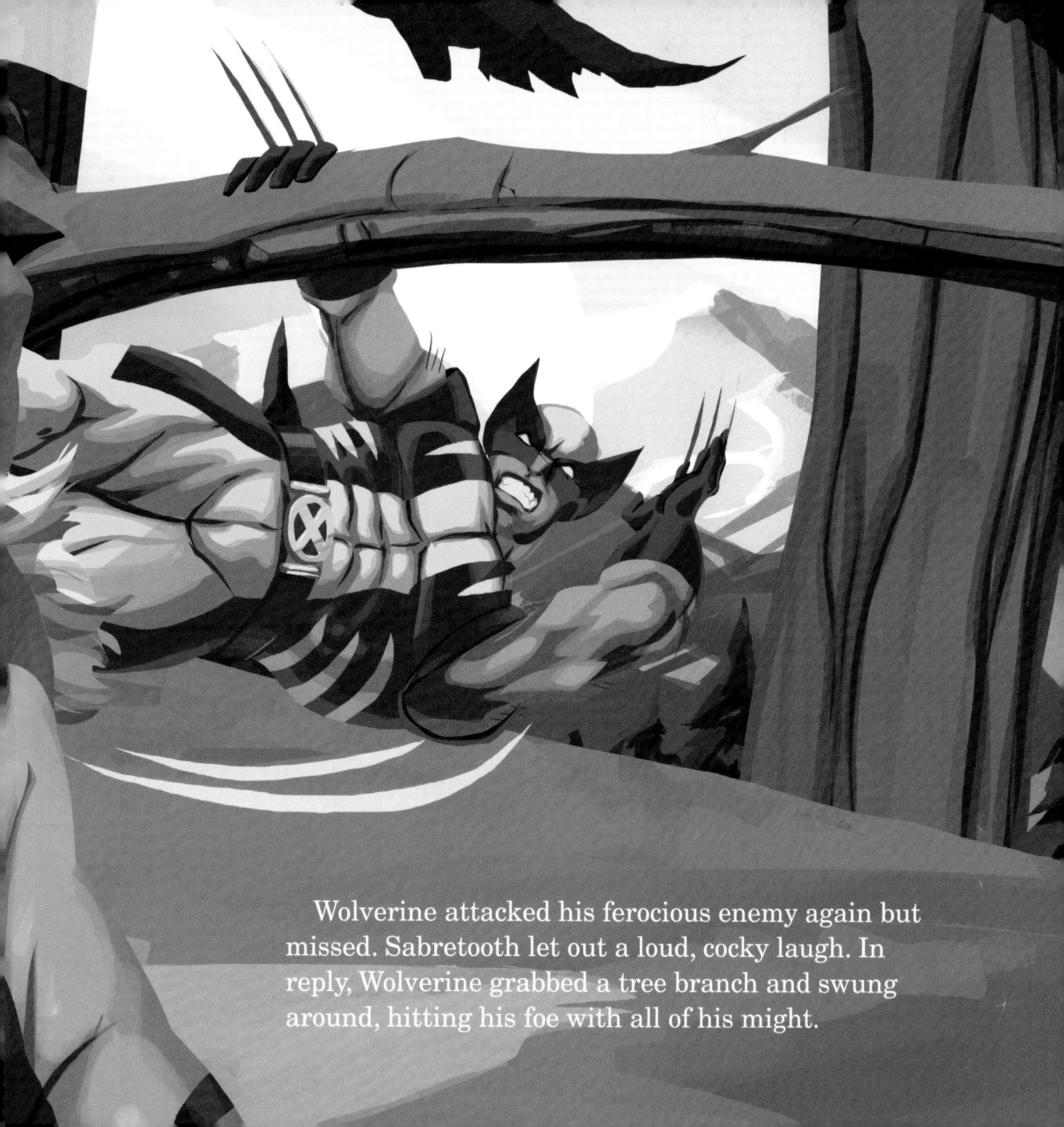

Wolverine attacked his ferocious enemy again but missed. Sabretooth let out a loud, cocky laugh. In reply, Wolverine grabbed a tree branch and swung around, hitting his foe with all of his might.

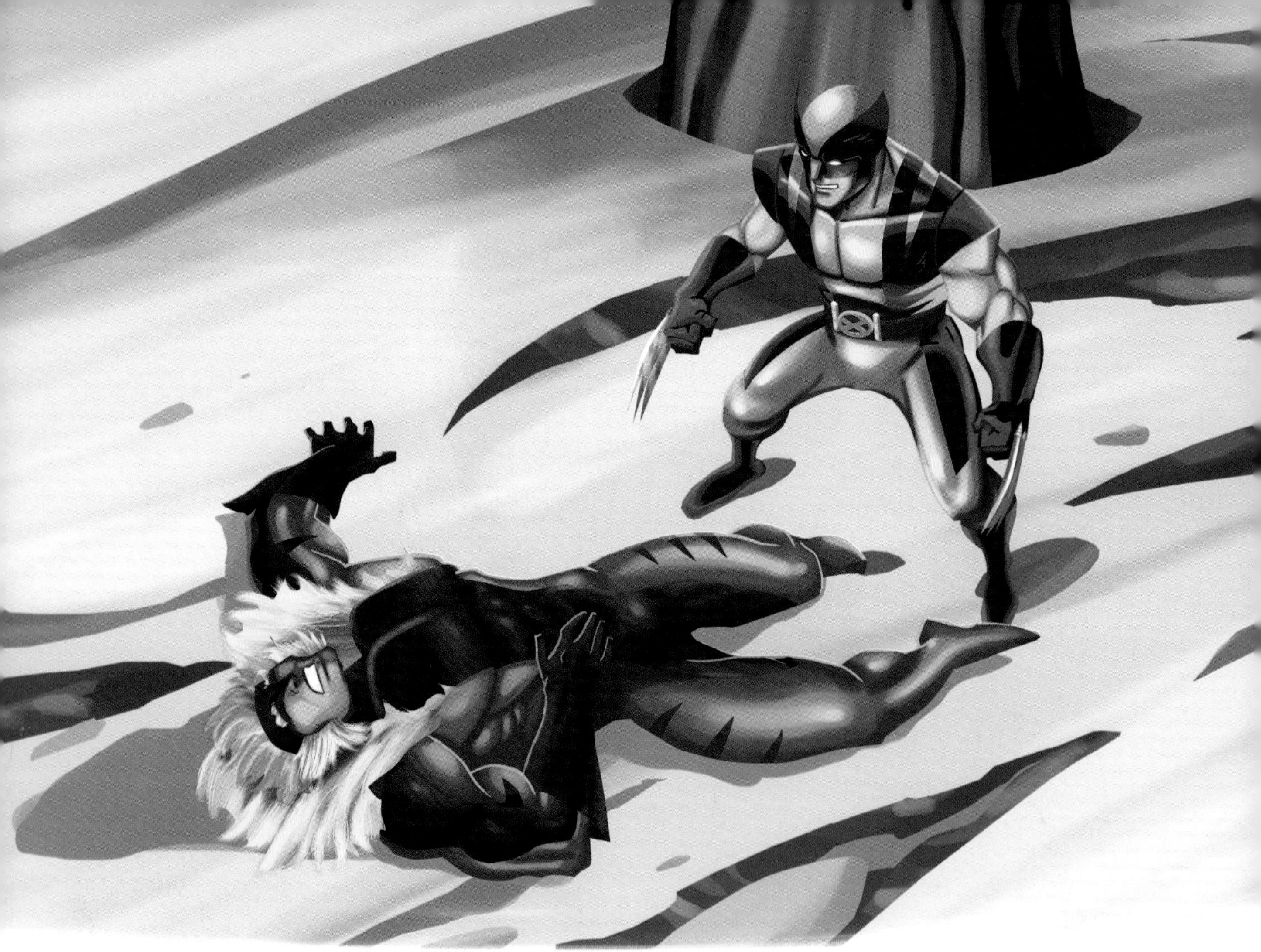

Sabretooth was knocked out! Wolverine looked down at his fallen rival. Slowly, Sabretooth opened his eyes.

"You didn't finish me off. . ." Sabretooth said with surprise.

Wolverine grabbed the defeated villain and pulled him up close. He could smell the wild energy in him. The violent and crazed look in his eyes was still there, even though he had been beaten. Wolverine knew Sabretooth was dangerous.

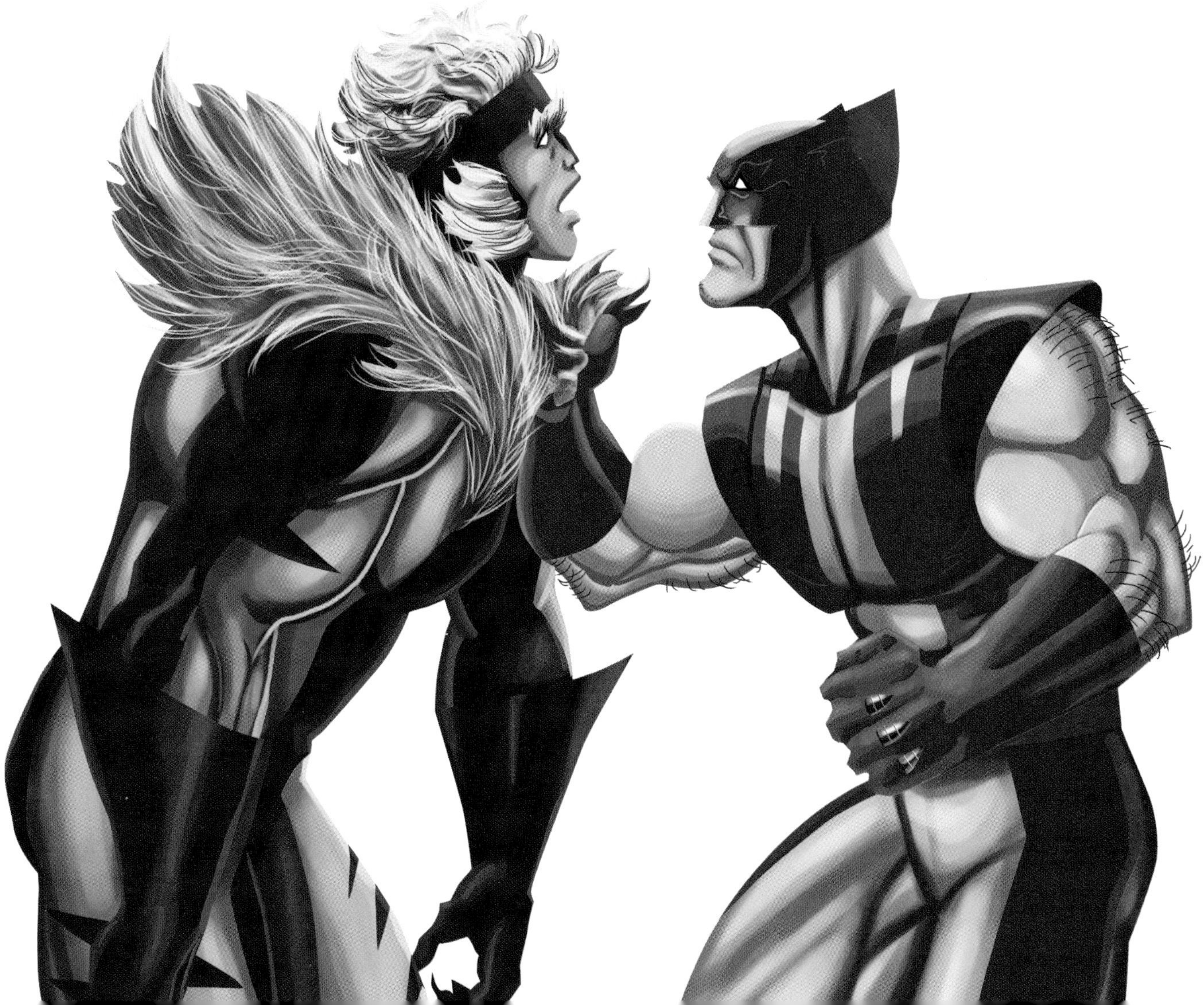

"I could," Wolverine said slowly, letting his claws out. "But I won't,"

"What? Why? I would have been merciless!" Now it was Sabretooth asking the questions.

"That's because you're an animal. **I am better than that.** Now if you would excuse me, I have somewhere to be," Wolverine said as he dropped Sabretooth **on** the ground.

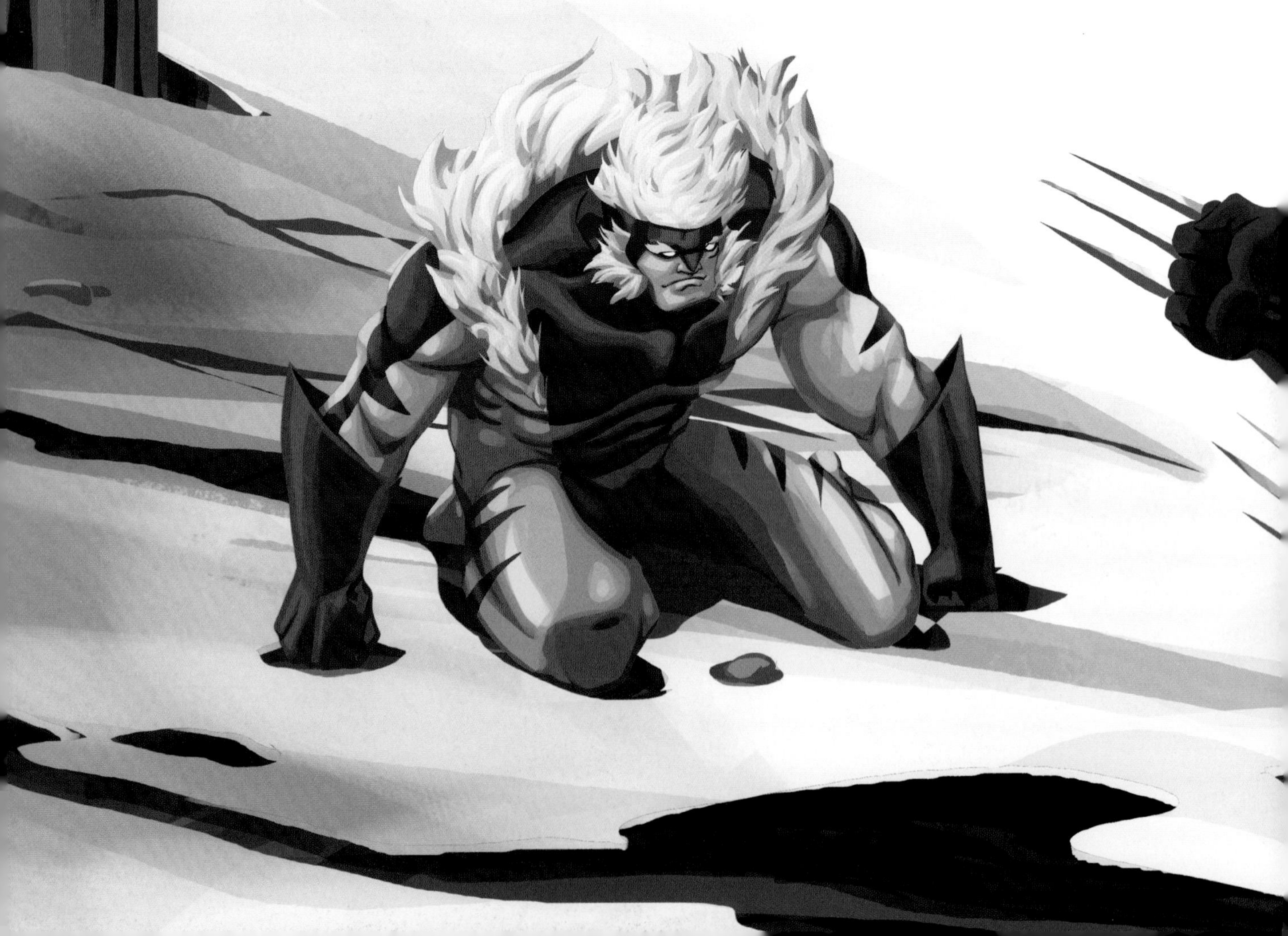

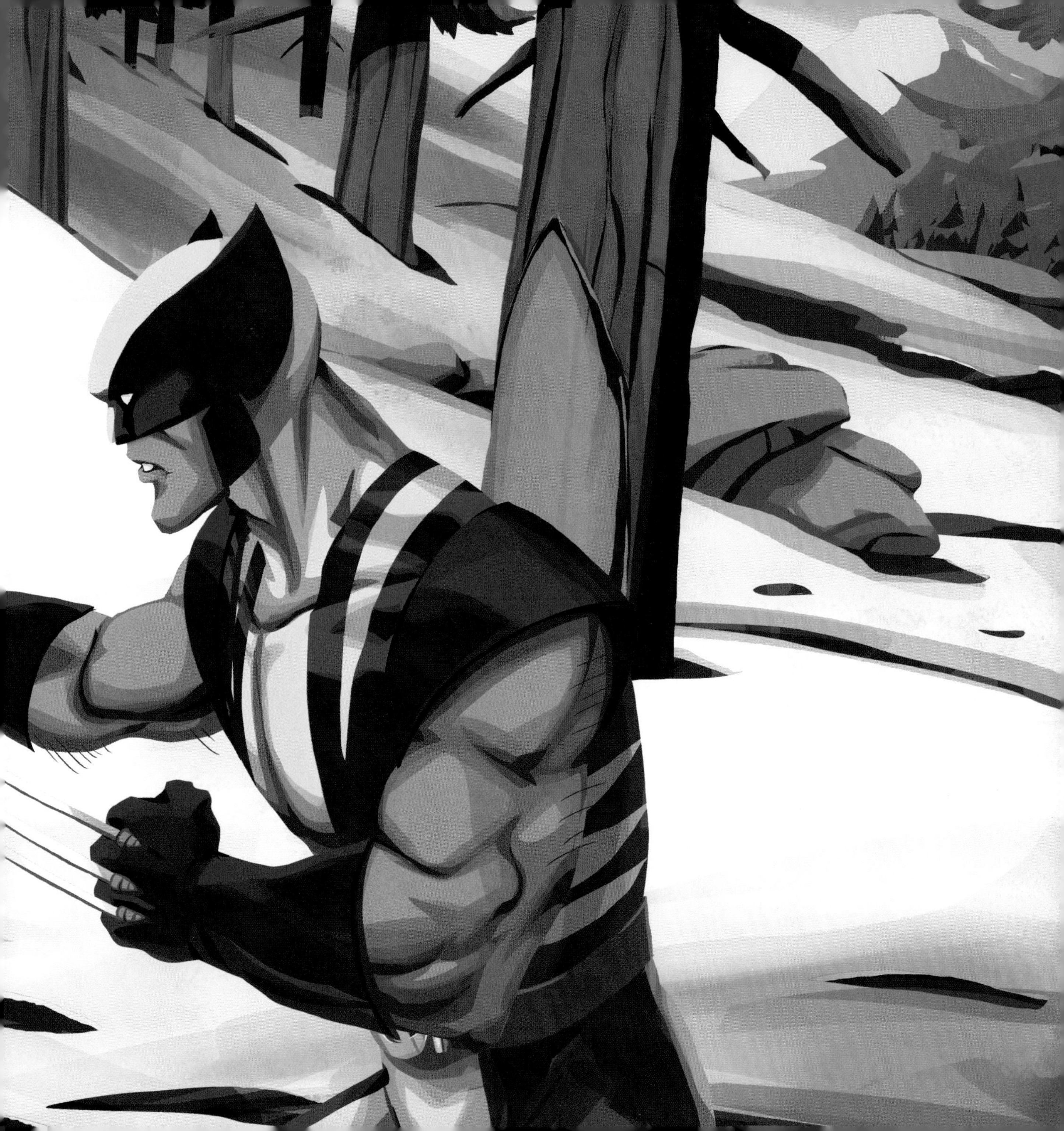

Wolverine thought about how he should have been spending his birthday with his friends the X-Men instead of wasting time fighting a crazy villain like Sabretooth. He realized he wanted to be with his friends, the people he truly cared about. He got on his motorcycle and raced back to the X-Mansion, **his home.**